ROMEO AND JULIET

By Jennifer Mulherin   *Illustrations by* George Thompson

CHERRYTREE BOOKS

Author's note
There is no substitute for seeing the plays of Shakespeare performed. Only then can you really understand why Shakespeare is our greatest dramatist and poet. This book simply gives you the background to the play and tells you about the story and characters. It will, I hope, encourage you to see the play.

A Cherrytree Book

Designed and produced by
A S Publishing

First published 1988
by Cherrytree Press Ltd
327 High Street
Slough
Berkshire SL1 1TX

Reprinted 1990, 1992, 1993 (twice), 1994, 1996, 1997
First softcover edition 1994
Reprinted 1995, 1996, 1998 (twice), 2000, 2001

Copyright this edition © Evans Brothers Ltd 2001

British Library Cataloguing in Publication Data
Mulherin, Jennifer
    Romeo and Juliet - (Shakespeare for everyone)
    1. Shakespeare, William, Romeo and Juliet - Juvenile literature
    I. Title II. Bancroft Hunt, Norman
    111. Series
    822.3'3 PR2831

ISBN 1 84234 057 3

Printed in Hong Kong through Colorcraft Ltd

Contents

Romeo and Juliet *and the theatre*

planities siue arena.

Ex obseruationibus Londinensibus Johannis de witt

This drawing made by an artist in Elizabethan times shows the interior of the Swan Theatre, a popular London playhouse in Shakespeare's day.

When Shakespeare was a boy, plays were performed in the courtyards of inns or sometimes in private houses or at court. In those days, there were no theatre buildings such as we have today. In fact, the first theatre in England was not built until 1576. Even then, it was very different from the ones we know today.

The wooden O

In *Henry V*, Shakespeare describes the famous Globe Theatre (built in 1599) as a 'wooden O'. This theatre, as well as other Elizabethan playhouses such as the Swan and the Fortune, was made of wood. And it was round in shape. Inside there was a paved courtyard which was open to the sky. The stage jutted out from the side of the building into this courtyard – so it was open on three sides.

Housing the audience

The yard surrounding the stage was called 'the pit'. People paid one penny for standing room in this area. About 800 spectators could watch the play from the pit. But some preferred to be more comfortable or to be protected from the weather. By paying more money, you could sit in one of the three covered tiers or galleries at the sides of the building. These overlooked the pit and the stage. And about 1500 people could be seated.

The arrangement of the stage

The open-sided stage was raised above ground level on stilts. The area under the stage was known as 'the hell'. It was often enclosed by a curtain and could be reached from the stage through trapdoors. Characters in the plays could descend or emerge onto the stage through these trapdoors.

Part of the stage was covered by a roof projecting from the wall at the back of the stage. The roof was held up at the front by two pillars. At the back of the stage, on either side, were two doors – and it was mainly through these that players made their entrances and exits. Between the doors was a small alcove or booth which was curtained off. This was called the 'discovery' area. In *Romeo and Juliet*, this would have been used as Juliet's bedroom. Towards the end of the play, after she has taken a sleeping draught, the curtain would be pulled across. Later, the nurse draws the curtain and discovers Juliet on her bed in a death-like trance.

Above the discovery area was a kind of gallery. Sometimes this was occupied by privileged spectators, sometimes by musicians, or used by the actors as a balcony. This is how it would have been used in *Romeo and Juliet*. Above this gallery was a kind of hut, used to represent, for example, the top of a city's walls or a room above the street. It could also house a machine for lowering actors onto the stage.

The areas backstage

The two doors at the back of the stage led to the 'tiring house'. This was the Elizabethan term for a dressing room. The area behind the balcony was also part of the tiring house. And at the back of the hut on the top, costumes and scenery would be stored.

The famous Globe Theatre in London's Southwark. It was built in 1599 and Shakespeare described it in one of his plays as the 'wooden O'.

GLOBE . SOUTHWARKE.

"our theaters are raf'd downe
and where they stood is coarse cotnyas
now are put of th
by wyvs of combmakyes
and mildwyvt of cowne.
Draven

5

Private theatres

Certain plays were acted at court or in private theatres. The audiences for these special performances usually consisted of wealthy or noble people. The plays were put on in a large rectangular room with a raised stage at one end. Artificial light could be used to create effects and up to 700 people were seated. These performances were usually staged to mark a special occasion, and rich costumes and music were often featured. Scholars believe, for example, that *A Midsummer Night's Dream* was first performed in a private theatre to celebrate a wedding. Some of Shakespeare's later plays, such as *The Winter's Tale* and *The Tempest* were almost certainly written for such a theatre. These plays have elaborate stage effects. And it was possible to achieve these in private theatres but not in public theatres.

Boy actors

In Shakespeare's time, women were barred by law from acting on the stage. Because of this, all the female parts in Shakespeare's plays were performed by young boys aged between eight and 13. This explains why, in many of Shakespeare's plays such as *Twelfth Night* and *As You Like It*, the main female character is disguised as a boy for much of the play in order to conceal her identity.

A continuous performance

Today, Shakespeare's plays are performed with elaborate sets and scene changes; in Shakespeare's own time they were performed without interruption and there was little scenery. Because of this, the characters often tell the audience what locality the stage is meant to be at different times. Or they mention what time of day it is to show that time has passed. In this way, the scenes are set with words and gestures rather than a lot of scenery.

Animal baiting, along with other sports and entertainments, took place in some theatres as well as plays.

A world famous love story

Almost everyone knows the story of *Romeo and Juliet*; it is one of the world's most famous love stories. It is frequently staged, and has been made into a film and adapted for the musical, *West Side Story*. *Romeo and Juliet* is the story of two 'star-crossed' young lovers, whose families are engaged in a bitter feud. The very first lines of the play tell us about this long-standing quarrel:

> *Two households, both alike in dignity*
> *(In fair Verona, where we lay our scene)*
> *From ancient grudge break into new mutiny,*

Romeo and Juliet fall instantly in love with each other. But because of their families' hatred, their happiness and youth are wasted. They die in the most tragic way.

The family feud

Shakespeare hardly ever invented the stories for his plays. Like other dramatists of his time, he borrowed them from old stories, poems or plays. *Romeo and Juliet* is based on a long poem written by an Englishman, Arthur Brooke, in 1562. But Brooke probably found the story in old French and Italian books and rewrote it. Shakespeare, in any case, added details of his own – and then put into it some of the most beautiful and poetic words he ever wrote.

What made Shakespeare think of this love story set against the background of a family feud? Well, at the time, there *was* a feud going on between the Danvers and the Long families in Wiltshire. Shakespeare knew about this quarrel because the Danvers were close friends of his patron, the Earl of Southampton.

This is a portrait of
Elizabeth Vernon, Countess
of Southampton – the wife
of Shakespeare's patron.
Her clothes show how richly
dressed young noblewomen,
such as Juliet, must have
been in Shakespeare's time.

This Italian painting shows a trio of performing musicians. Small groups like this were often hired to provide music for banquets, balls and other special occasions.

Was Shakespeare in love?

About the time of *Romeo and Juliet*, Shakespeare was also writing his *Sonnets*. Many of these are love poems. Some describe the agony of love which is not returned. Shakespeare was about 30 years old at the time, so he was not young like Romeo and Juliet. But scholars believe that he was in love – with a dark, musical lady. So maybe he was drawing on his own feelings when he was writing this heart-breaking story.

The references to music

Shakespeare makes more references to music in *Romeo and Juliet* than in any play he had written before. Almost a whole scene is given to the musicians who had been hired to play at Juliet's wedding banquet to Romeo's rival, Paris. And there are mentions of particular songs and ballads which were popular at the time. Why did Shakespeare make so much of music in this play? We know that the Dark Lady of the *Sonnets* was an expert player of the virginals (an early type of keyboard instrument, popular with lady musicians, including Elizabeth I). Perhaps that is why.

The stupidity of age

There is no doubt that Shakespeare understood the feelings of Romeo and Juliet. He makes us see love as they see it. It is their parents – with their quarrels and feuds – who do not understand. Their cold-heartedness and stupidity are the real cause of the tragic deaths of the young lovers. Romeo and Juliet are innocent victims who had the bad luck to be born into families that hate each other.

The beauty of youthful love

Romeo and Juliet ought not to have died. And it is not much consolation that their families are reconciled at the end. But in a way, they do live. Shakespeare has created a masterpiece that will keep their simple sad story alive forever. It is one of the greatest celebrations of young love ever written. Lovers everywhere recognize how Romeo and Juliet felt, and respond to Shakespeare's exquisite expression of those feelings. The play tells a sad story. But when we hear the names Romeo and Juliet we think at once of a great love story, not a tragedy.

This engraving shows a lady playing the virginals in the company of other musicians. Both Elizabeth 1 and Shakespeare's Dark Lady played this instrument well.

10

The story of Romeo and Juliet

In Verona in Italy, a long-standing feud exists between two families – the Montagues and the Capulets. When their servants meet in the street, they quarrel, and this is how the play opens – with a street brawl.

A street battle
Benvolio who is a Montague tries to stop the fight. But Tybalt, who is a Capulet, will not listen. The quarrel turns into a violent battle. This alarms the citizens of Verona – and their ruler, Prince Escalius. The Prince stops the battle. But he declares that any more fighting between the families will be punished by death.

The love-sick Romeo
Benvolio's cousin, Romeo, is unhappy. And his parents are worried about him. Benvolio finds out that Romeo is in love. But the lady does not return his love. Benvolio tells him to look for another lady. But Romeo, of course, says he can never love anyone else.

> **Romeo on the nature of love**
> *Love is a smoke rais'd with the fume of sighs;*
> *Being purg'd, a fire sparkling in lovers' eyes;*
> *Being vex'd, a sea raging with lovers' tears;*
> *What is it else? a madness most discreet,*
> *A choking gall and a preserving sweet.*
> Act 1 Sc i

A proposal of marriage
Juliet's father is Lord Capulet. He has been asked for Juliet's hand in marriage by Count Paris. Although she is very young, Lord Capulet agrees to the marriage – but only if Juliet decides she wants to marry the handsome young Count. He invites Paris to a ball he is giving that night, and

sends his servant off to invite other guests. Unfortunately, the servant has never learned to read. So when he meets Romeo and Benvolio in the street, he asks them to read out the list for him.

Why Romeo goes to the ball

One of the guests is Rosaline, the lady with whom Romeo is hopelessly in love. Romeo agrees to gatecrash the ball with Benvolio – but only to catch a glimpse of Rosaline.

Juliet hears of the marriage proposal

Lady Capulet tells Juliet and her Nurse about Paris's marriage proposal. She tells Juliet to look for him at the ball. And to notice how handsome he is. Juliet replies that, if she likes him, she will consider marrying him.

Romeo and his friends go to the ball

Romeo and his friends, Benvolio and Mercutio, wear masks to the ball. (This was common in Shakespeare's time.) Romeo is worried that he will be recognized as a Montague. And he is also troubled by a strange fear, because of a dream he has had. But Mercutio jokes about the dream. He says it was caused by the fairy Queen Mab.

At the Capulets' house, the music and dancing has already begun. Romeo, who decides not to dance, notices Juliet. He immediately thinks how beautiful she is. But just then Romeo is recognized by Tybalt. He is furious that a Montague is at the ball. He wants to kill Romeo. But he is stopped from doing anything by Juliet's father who sternly tells Tybalt to behave himself.

Romeo meets Juliet

When the dance ends, Romeo goes up to Juliet. He touches her hand and they begin to talk. They fall instantly in love

with each other, and kiss – just before they are parted by the Nurse. She tells Romeo that Juliet is the daughter of the house. Horrified, Romeo realizes that he has fallen in love with a Capulet. And he hurries away from the ball with Benvolio. As the guests leave, Juliet asks the Nurse about Romeo. She learns that he is the Montagues' only son. She, too, is struck with horror.

Lady Capulet describes Paris
This precious book of love, this unbound lover,
To beautify him, only lacks a cover:

Act I Sc iii

Queen Mab's carriage
Her chariot is an empty hazelnut,
Made by the joiner squirrel or old grub,
Time out o' mind the fairies' coachmakers.
And in this state she gallops night by night
Through lovers' brains, and then they dream of love;

Act I Sc iv

13

Juliet on the balcony

After the ball is over, Romeo escapes from his friends. Jumping over the wall into the Capulets' orchard, he sees Juliet on a balcony. He is dazzled by her beauty. She does not know that Romeo can see and hear her. And she declares her love for him – even though his name is Montague.

Romeo on seeing Juliet on the balcony
But soft! what light through yonder window breaks?
It is the east, and Juliet is the sun!
. . . her eyes in heaven
Would through the airy region stream so bright
That birds would sing and think it were not night.   Act II Sc ii

Juliet on Romeo's name
O Romeo, Romeo! wherefore art thou Romeo?
. . . O, be some other name!
What's in a name? that which we call a rose
By any other name would smell as sweet;   Act II Sc ii

Romeo and Juliet declare their love

Romeo calls to Juliet. And she recognizes his voice. He swears his love for her – and she for him – in the most beautiful words. They agree to marry the next day. But they can hardly bear to part.

Romeo swears his love
Lady, by yonder blessed moon I swear,
That tips with silver all these fruit-tree tops, –

Juliet declares her love
My bounty is as boundless as the sea,
My love as deep; the more I give to thee,
The more I have, for both are infinite.
          Act II Sc ii

Juliet's parting words
Good-night, good-night! parting is such sweet sorrow
That I shall say good-night till it be morrow.

Act II Sc ii

Romeo arranges the marriage

As dawn breaks, Romeo goes to see his father confessor, Friar Laurence. The priest is surprised that Romeo is now in love with Juliet. But he agrees to marry the lovers. He hopes it might reconcile their families.

Meanwhile Mercutio and Benvolio have been looking for Romeo. They know he did not come home the night before. Tybalt has sent a letter challenging him to a duel. When Romeo appears, he is in a cheerful mood. He jokes with his friends. Then he asks Juliet's Nurse to tell her about the wedding. It is to be that afternoon.

The marriage ceremony

Juliet has been waiting anxiously for the Nurse to return. The Nurse is a silly woman. She chatters on before telling Juliet the time of the wedding. Juliet is delighted, and she rushes off to meet Romeo and the Friar.

Friar Laurence is ready to perform the marriage ceremony. But he is uneasy. He warns Romeo about hasty marriages. It seems as if he is prophesying the lovers' tragic deaths. But the wedding takes place. And Romeo and Juliet arrange to see each other that night.

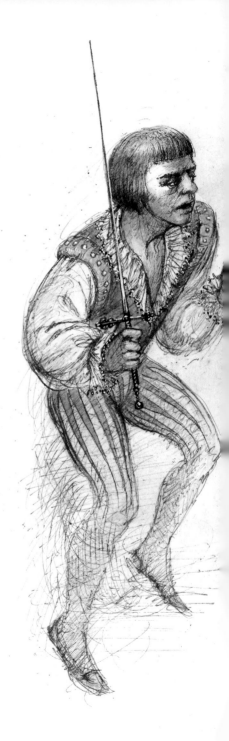

The Friar's warning
These violent delights have violent ends,
And in their triumph die . . .
Therefore, love moderately; long love doth so;

Act II Sc vi

A fatal duel takes place

Mercutio and Benvolio are walking in the street when they meet Tybalt. He is looking for Romeo. He is still angry that Romeo went to the Capulet ball. Just then, Romeo arrives. Tybalt insults him and calls him a villain. But Romeo does not want to fight. Juliet's family are like his own now he is

16

married. But Mercutio is furious. He thinks Romeo is a coward. He draws his sword and attacks Tybalt. Romeo urges them to stop. But as he tries to break them apart, Tybalt stabs Mercutio to death.

Romeo gets his revenge

Romeo is grief stricken at Mercutio's death. He died defending Romeo. Romeo seeks out Tybalt, and they fight a duel. Tybalt is killed. Prince Escalius hears of the murders. He banishes Romeo from Verona instead of ordering his execution. But this is small comfort for Romeo.

Juliet learns of Romeo's banishment

Meanwhile, Juliet is longing for night to come, when Romeo is to visit her.

Juliet longs for nightfall
Come, gentle night, come, loving, black-brow'd night,
Give me my Romeo; and, when he shall die,
Take him and cut him out in little stars,
And he will make the face of heaven so fine,
That all the world will be in love with night,

Act III Sc ii

17

Just then, her Nurse rushes in with the news of Tybalt's death and Romeo's banishment. Juliet is full of sorrow. Her meeting with Romeo will be a last farewell.

Since the fight, Romeo has been hiding with Friar Laurence. When the Nurse brings him news of Juliet's unhappiness, he is very upset, and wants to kill himself. But the Friar urges him to see Juliet – and then to leave for Mantua.

Lord Capulet arranges a marriage

Paris still wishes to marry Juliet. Now suddenly Lord Capulet agrees to the wedding – but without asking Juliet about her feelings. He arranges for it to take place in three days' time.

Romeo and Juliet's farewell

Romeo has secretly spent the night with Juliet. As dawn breaks, he knows he must hurry away – or else be captured.

At the break of day

> Jul. *Wilt thou be gone? it is not yet near day;*
> *It was the nightingale, and not the lark,*
> *That pierc'd the fearful hollow of thine ear;*
> *Nightly she sings on yon pomegranate-tree:*
> *Believe me, love, it was the nightingale.*
>   Rom. *It was the lark, the herald of the morn,*
> *No nightingale: look, love, what envious streaks*
> *Do lace the severing clouds in yonder east:*
> *Night's candles are burnt out, and jocund day*
> *Stands tiptoe on the misty mountain tops:*

Act III Sc v

Romeo's and Juliet's farewell

Rom. *Farewell, farewell! one kiss, and I'll descend.*
Jul *Art thou gone so? my lord, my love, my friend!*
I must hear from thee every day in the hour,
For in a minute there are many days:
O! by this count I shall be much in years
Ere I again behold my Romeo.

Act III Sc v

The lovers find it difficult to part. But as Romeo climbs down the balcony, they bid each other farewell.

Juliet refuses to marry Paris

Just as Romeo leaves, Juliet learns from her mother that she is to marry Paris in three days' time. Juliet is angry and refuses to marry the Count. When her father hears this, he is furious. He tells Juliet she is proud and ungrateful. He orders her to marry Paris – or else be dragged to the church.

19

Lord Capulet's threat

Look to 't, think on 't, I do not use to jest.
Thursday is near; lay hand on heart, advise:
An you be mine, I'll give you to my friend;
An you be not, hang, beg, starve, die in the streets.
For, by my soul, I'll ne'er acknowledge thee,
Nor what is mine shall never do thee good:

Act III Sc v

Juliet appeals to her mother. She asks her to delay the marriage. But her mother refuses to listen. In desperation, Juliet asks the Nurse's advice. The woman cheerfully says Juliet should marry Paris. She points out that Romeo is not

likely to return. Juliet realizes that everyone is against her. She decides to ask Friar Laurence to help.

The Friar's plan to stop the marriage

Juliet tells the Friar that she cannot marry Paris. She would rather kill herself, she says. Seeing her so desperate, the priest makes a plan. He knows of a sleeping potion which can make a person appear dead. But after some time, the person who takes it wakes up – just as if they had been asleep. The Friar tells Juliet to agree to marry Paris. After she has taken the potion, her family will think she is dead. She will be placed in a tomb. But when she wakes, Romeo will be with her. Then they can both flee to Mantua. Friar Laurence says he will tell Romeo the plan by letter – so that Romeo can come back to Verona in secret. Juliet agrees to the plan and goes home.

The wedding preparations

Juliet tells her father that she will marry Paris. Lord Capulet is delighted, so much so that he brings the wedding forward by a day! Will this upset the Friar's plan? In great excitement Capulet goes off to make the preparations for the wedding. Juliet and her Nurse decide on the wedding clothes. Then Juliet sends both her Nurse and her mother away. She tells them she wants to pray before the marriage ceremony. But really, she is plucking up her courage to take the sleeping potion.

Juliet is frightened

Juliet knows she must now swallow the sleeping potion. But she is very frightened. 'I have a faint cold fear thrills through my veins, That almost freezes up the heat of life,' she says. She worries that the potion may not work. Will she wake up before Romeo arrives? Will she see Tybalt's dead body? Will spirits haunt the tomb? But for Romeo's sake she *must* take the potion. She lies on her bed. Then she swallows the mixture. She falls back as the bottle drops from her hand.

How Juliet is found dead

The time has come to dress for the wedding ceremony. The Nurse goes to wake Juliet. She draws the curtain. But Juliet does not wake up when she calls. She now realizes that the girl is dead. She screams for help. And then the Capulets rush in – followed by the Friar and Paris. Juliet's parents pour out their grief. They are interrupted by the Friar. He knows, of course, that Juliet is not really dead. He says they must arrange for the burial and carry Juliet's body to the church.

Capulet on Juliet's death
Her blood is settled, and her joints are stiff;
Life and these lips have long been separated.
Death lies on her like an untimely frost
Upon the sweetest flower of all the field.

Act IV Sc v

What happens to Romeo in Mantua

In Mantua, Romeo has a dream that Juliet finds him dead. In fact, he learns from his servant that Juliet is dead. He decides to go at once to Verona. He buys some poison. When he arrives, he intends to kill himself in the vault where Juliet lies.

How the Friar's plan goes awry

Back in Verona, the Friar learns that his letter to Romeo was never delivered. His messenger was prevented by plague from leaving Verona. Juliet is to wake up in three hours – so Friar Laurence hurries off to the tomb.

The Friar's advice to the Capulets

She's not well married that lives married long,
But she's best married that dies married young.
Dry up your tears, and stick your rosemary
On this fair corse and, as the custom is,
In all her best array bear her to church:　　　Act IV Sc v

Romeo's dream in Mantua

I dreamt my lady came and found me dead –
Strange dream, that gives a dead man leave to think!
And breath'd such life with kisses in my lips,
That I reviv'd and was an emperor.

Act V Sc i

Romeo and Paris meet at Juliet's tomb

Paris is mourning at Juliet's tomb when he spies Romeo. He thinks he is there for evil purposes. He challenges Romeo, and they fight a duel. Only after he falls, does Romeo realize he has killed Paris.

The death of Romeo

Romeo opens Juliet's tomb. He gazes lovingly on his bride.

> **Romeo gazes on Juliet**
> *. . . Ah, dear Juliet,*
> *Why art thou yet so fair? Shall I believe*
> *That unsubstantial death is amorous,*
> *And that the lean abhorred monster keeps*
> *Thee here in dark to be his paramour?*
>
> Act v Sc iii

Romeo then prepares himself to die.

> **Romeo's last kiss**
> *. . . Eyes, look your last!*
> *Arms, take your last embrace! and, lips, O you*
> *The doors of breath, seal with a righteous kiss . . .*
>
> Act v Sc iii

He drinks the poison and dies.

Juliet awakes

Just as Juliet wakes up, the Friar arrives. He sees the bodies of Paris and Romeo. He tells Juliet they must fly away at once. When Juliet realizes that Romeo is dead, she refuses to leave. She sees that he has taken poison. 'O churl! drink all, and leave no friendly drop To help me after?' she says. She kisses his lips. Then she takes up Romeo's dagger to stab herself. Just as she does, she hears noise outside. Paris's servant has summoned help.

The bodies are discovered

The servant has summoned the help of a watchman. They enter the tomb and find the bodies of Romeo, Paris and Juliet. They send a messenger to bring the Prince and the Capulets and Montagues to the tomb. The Friar has been

arrested in the churchyard. He is trembling and sorrowful. And he is suspected of the murders.

Just then, the Prince arrives. He is followed by the Capulets. They are horrified to see Juliet stabbed and bleeding. When Lord Montague appears, he too is shocked and grief-stricken.

The Friar explains the tragedy

The Prince demands to know what has happened. The Friar begins to explain how the events took place. He partly blames himself for the lovers' deaths. He tells how he married Romeo and Juliet. Then he describes how the lovers were affected by Tybalt's death and Romeo's banishment. He explains the plan he hatched. And how his letter failed to reach Romeo in Mantua. Then he offers to die himself – for taking part in the tragedy.

The Friar offers to die

. . . if aught in this
Miscarried by my fault, let my old life
Be sacrific'd some hour before his time
Unto the rigour of severest law.

Act v Sc iii

The story is confirmed by Romeo's servant

Romeo's servant explains how he broke the news of Juliet's death and how he and Romeo set off at once for Verona. Still in his hand he carried a letter from Romeo to his father.

Romeo's letter confirms all that has been said. And the Prince decides that nobody will be punished for the deaths. Everybody, he says, has suffered enough. But he does put the blame for the tragedy on the Capulet and Montague feud.

The Prince blames the Capulets and Montagues

. . . Capulet! Montague!
See, what a scourge is laid upon your hate,
That heaven finds means to kill your joys with love,
And I, for winking at your discords too,
Have lost a brace of kinsmen: all are punish'd.

Act v Sc iii

The Montagues and Capulets are reconciled

The Montagues and Capulets now agree that their feud is over. And they declare they will build statues to honour the lovers. The Prince speaks the last words of tribute to the lovers.

The Prince on the story of Romeo and Juliet.

Go hence, to have more talk of these sad things;
Some shall be pardon'd and some punished:
For never was a story of more woe
Than this of Juliet and her Romeo.

Act v Sc iii

The play's characters

Juliet

Juliet

Juliet is a young girl, only 14 years of age. She is a gentle person and obedient to her parents. And she is fond of the Nurse who has looked after her since she was a baby. She belongs to a noble family from Verona. Her cousin is the quick-tempered young man, Tybalt. Probably because she is so young, Juliet does not have friends outside her family. This is a shame – because when her family force her to marry Paris she has no young person to turn to for advice.

In a way, falling in love makes Juliet more grown-up. Now she does not rely on her parents, but makes up her own mind. Her first thoughts are for Romeo. After Romeo is banished, she does not beg him to stay. This is because she knows he will be captured. Her love for Romeo becomes the most important thing in life. In the end, she prefers to die rather than live her life without him.

Romeo

Romeo is a person who rushes into things without thinking. When he hears that Juliet is dead, he sets off straight away for Verona. And we know he has bought poison to kill himself. But he is a kind-hearted, good man. He did not want to kill Tybalt. He is generous and kind to his friends and his servant. And when he kills Paris, he feels very sad.

Falling in love with Juliet helps Romeo to grow up. At the beginning of the play, he feels sorry for himself. But at the end, he thinks of Juliet and not himself. When he kills himself it is to be reunited with her.

Romeo

Lord and Lady Capulet

Lord Capulet is a stubborn old man. And he can also be short-tempered. He loves his only daughter and wants the best for her.

Lady Capulet is much younger than her husband. She is an aristocratic lady, and not very warm-hearted. Although she probably loves Juliet, she is not as close to her as the Nurse is. She thinks it is best for Juliet to marry a suitable person like Paris, even if she does not love him. She hates Romeo and plans to poison him after he has killed Tybalt. She keeps the feud going more than her husband.

Mercutio

Tybalt

A visit from Queen Mab
Sometimes she gallops o'er a
courtier's nose,
And then dreams he of smelling
out a suit;
And sometimes comes she with a
tithe-pig's tail
Tickling a parson's nose as a' lies
asleep,
Then dreams he of another
benefice;
Act I Sc iii

Mercutio

Mercutio is one of the most likeable characters in the play, He is young and lively. And he is always talking and joking. He teases Romeo about being in love with Rosaline.

He is also loyal and honourable. When Romeo is insulted by Tybalt, he springs to his defence. Even as he dies from the wounds inflicted by Tybalt's sword, he is brave. He pretends that it is only 'a scratch'. His death is one of the saddest parts of the play.

Tybalt

Tybalt is a quarrelsome young man. He is a troublemaker who loves fighting. He is very angry when Romeo appears at the Capulets' ball. He wants to fight him straight away. He is only prevented from doing this by Juliet's father. More than anyone else, he is the person who keeps the feud between the Montagues and the Capulets alive. He likes violence for its own sake. When he is killed by Romeo, we are not particularly sorry.

Lord and Lady Capulet

29

Juliet suspects the Friar
What if it be a poison which the Friar
Subtly hath ministered to have me dead,
Lest in this marriage he should be dishonoured
Because he married me before to Romeo?

Act IV Sc iii

Friar Laurence   The Nurse   Paris

Friar Laurence

Friar Laurence is a wise and holy man. He is a priest and the person to whom both Romeo and Juliet turn to for advice. And usually, he gives them good advice. Some people say, though, that he should not have married the lovers in secret. They say that it was wrong to deceive the parents of Romeo and Juliet. For a moment, even Juliet thinks the Friar regrets his part in the marriage. She thinks the sleeping potion he gave her may be a poison.

The Friar tells of his part in the tragic events. Perhaps he could have prevented them, he says. He is willing to be punished by the Prince if he is found guilty. But the Prince admires his honesty – and pardons him. Like the Montagues and Capulets, Friar Laurence has suffered enough for his part in the tragedy.

The Nurse

Juliet's Nurse is a down-to-earth, rather stupid woman. She nursed Juliet as a baby and still fusses over her. She loves her like her own child. Juliet is very fond of the Nurse. She confides in her – telling her about Romeo and the wedding. But when Romeo is banished, the Nurse advises Juliet to marry Paris. This is the sensible thing to do, she tells Juliet. Juliet is shocked. She realizes that the Nurse does not understand how deep her love for Romeo is. Sadly, she is unable to talk to her any more about her feelings.

Paris

Paris is a handsome young man, pleasant and courteous. Because he is a cousin of the Prince of Verona, he is a most eligible suitor for Juliet. He courts her in the correct way – by asking permission from her father. Paris seems to truly care for Juliet. He sorrowfully mourns at her grave. He is also brave when he approaches Romeo at the tomb and dies in the fight. Romeo is saddened at his death. He knows that Paris was an honourable man.

The life and plays of Shakespeare

Life of Shakespeare

1564 William Shakespeare born at Stratford-upon-Avon.

1582 Shakespeare marries Anne Hathaway, eight years his senior.

1583 Shakespeare's daughter, Susanna, is born.

1585 The twins, Hamnet and Judith, are born.

1587 Shakespeare goes to London.

1591-2 Shakespeare writes *The Comedy of Errors*. He is becoming well-known as an actor and writer.

1592 Theatres closed because of plague.

1593-4 Shakespeare writes *Titus Andronicus* and *The Taming of the Shrew*: he is member of the theatrical company, the Chamberlain's Men.

1594-5 Shakespeare writes *Romeo and Juliet*.

1595 Shakespeare writes *A Midsummer Night's Dream*.

1595-6 Shakespeare writes *Richard II*.

1596 Shakespeare's son, Hamnet, dies. He writes *King John* and *The Merchant of Venice*.

1597 Shakespeare buys New Place in Stratford.

1597-8 Shakespeare writes *Henry IV*.

1599 Shakespeare's theatre company opens the Globe Theatre.

1599-1600 Shakespeare writes *As You Like It*, *Henry V* and *Twelfth Night*.

1600-01 Shakespeare writes *Hamlet*.

1602-03 Shakespeare writes *All's Well That Ends Well*.

1603 Elizabeth I dies. James I becomes king. Theatres closed because of plague.

1603-04 Shakespeare writes *Othello*.

1605 Theatres closed because of plague.

1605-06 Shakespeare writes *Macbeth* and *King Lear*.

1606-07 Shakespeare writes *Antony and Cleopatra*.

1607 Susanna Shakespeare marries Dr John Hall. Theatres closed because of plague.

1608 Shakespeare's granddaughter, Elizabeth Hall, is born.

1609 *Sonnets* published. Theatres closed because of plague.

1610 Theatres closed because of plague. Shakespeare gives up his London lodgings and retires to Stratford.

1611-12 Shakespeare writes *The Tempest*.

1613 Globe Theatre burns to the ground during a performance of Henry VIII.

1616 Shakespeare dies on 23 April.

Shakespeare's plays

The Comedy of Errors
Love's Labour's Lost
Henry VI Part 2
Henry VI Part 3
Henry VI Part 1
Richard III
Titus Andronicus
The Taming of the Shrew
The Two Gentlemen of Verona
Romeo and Juliet
Richard II
A Midsummer Night's Dream
King John
The Merchant of Venice
Henry IV Part 1
Henry IV Part 2
Much Ado About Nothing
Henry V
Julius Caesar
As You Like It
Twelfth Night
Hamlet
The Merry Wives of Windsor
Troilus and Cressida
All's Well That Ends Well
Othello
Measure for Measure
King Lear
Macbeth
Antony and Cleopatra
Timon of Athens
Coriolanus
Pericles
Cymbeline
The Winter's Tale
The Tempest
Henry VIII

Index

Numerals in *italics* refer to picture captions.

Acknowledgements
The publishers would like to thank Morag Gibson for her help in producing this book.

Picture credits
p.8 In the collection of The Duke of Buccleuch, K.T., at Boughton House, Kettering, England. p.9 Reproduced by courtesy of the Trustees, The National Gallery, London. p.10 BBC Hulton Picture Library.